A. A. MILNE

Pooh Invents
a New Game

illustrated by
E. H. SHEPARD

DUTTON CHILDREN'S BOOKS

Pooh Invents a New Game

By the time it came to the edge of the Forest
the stream had grown up, so that it was
almost a river, and, being grown-up, it did
not run and jump and sparkle along as it used
to do when it was younger, but moved more
slowly. For it knew now where it was going,
and it said to itself, 'There is no hurry.
We shall get there some day.' But all the
little streams higher up in the Forest went
this way and that, quickly, eagerly, having
so much to find out before it was too late.

There was a broad track, almost as broad as a road, leading from the Outland to the Forest, but before it could come to the Forest, it had to cross this river. So, where it crossed, there was a wooden bridge, almost as broad as a road, with wooden rails on each side of it. Christopher Robin could just get his chin on to the top rail, if he wanted to, but it was more fun to stand on the bottom rail, so that he could lean right over, and watch the river slipping slowly away beneath him. Pooh could get his chin on to the bottom rail if he wanted to, but it was more fun to lie down and get his head under it, and watch the river slipping slowly away beneath him. And this was the only way in which Piglet and Roo could watch the river at all, because they were too small to reach the bottom rail. So they would lie down and watch it . . . and it slipped away very slowly, being in no hurry to get there.

One day, when Pooh was walking towards this

bridge, he was trying to make up a piece of poetry about fir-cones, because there they were, lying about on each side of him, and he felt singy. So he picked a fir-cone up, and looked at it, and said to himself, 'This is a very good fir-cone, and something ought to rhyme to it.' But he couldn't think of anything. And then this came into his head suddenly:

> Here is a myst'ry
> About a little fir-tree.
> Owl says it's *his* tree,
> And Kanga says it's *her* tree.

'Which doesn't make sense,' said Pooh, 'because Kanga doesn't live in a tree.'

He had just come to the bridge; and not looking where he was going, he tripped over something, and the fir-cone jerked out of his paw into the river.

'Bother,' said Pooh, as it floated slowly under the bridge, and he went back to get another fir-cone which had a rhyme to it.

But then he thought that he would just look
at the river instead, because it was a
peaceful sort of day, so he lay down and
looked at it, and it slipped slowly away
beneath him . . . and suddenly, there was his
fir-cone slipping away too.

'That's funny,' said Pooh. 'I dropped it
on the other side,' said Pooh, 'and it came out
on this side! I wonder if it would do it
again?' And he went back for some more fir-
cones.

It did. It kept on doing it. Then he
dropped two in at once, and leant over the

bridge to see which of them would come out
first; and one of them did; but as they were
both the same size, he didn't know if it was
the one which he wanted to win, or the other
one. So the next time he dropped one big one
and one little one, and the big one came out
first, which was what he had said it would do,
and the little one came out last, which was
what he had said it would do, so he had won
twice . . . and when he went home for tea, he had
won thirty-six and lost twenty-eight, which
meant that he was—that he had—well, you take
twenty-eight from thirty-six, and *that's* what
he was. Instead of the other way round.

And that was the beginning of the game
called Poohsticks, which Pooh invented, and
which he and his friends used to play on the
edge of the Forest. But they played with
sticks instead of fir-cones, because they were
easier to mark.

Now one day Pooh and Piglet and Rabbit and
Roo were all playing Poohsticks together. They

had dropped their sticks
in when Rabbit said
'Go!' and then they had
hurried across to the
other side of the bridge,
and now they were all
leaning over the edge, waiting to see whose
stick would come out first. But it was a long
time coming, because the river was very lazy
that day, and hardly seemed to mind if it didn't
ever get there at all.

'I can see mine!' cried Roo. 'No, I can't.
It's something else. Can you see yours, Piglet?
I thought I could see mine, but I couldn't.
There it is! No, it isn't. Can you see
yours, Pooh?'

'No,' said Pooh.

'I expect my stick's stuck,' said Roo.
'Rabbit, my stick's stuck. Is your stick
stuck, Piglet?'

'They always take longer than you think,'
said Rabbit.

'How long do you *think* they'll take?' asked Roo.

'I can see yours, Piglet,' said Pooh suddenly.

'Mine's a sort of greyish one,' said Piglet, not daring to lean too far over in case he fell in.

'Yes, that's what I can see. It's coming over on to my side.'

Rabbit leant over further than ever, looking for his and Roo wriggled up and down, calling out 'Come on, stick! Stick, stick, stick!' and Piglet got very excited because his was the only one which had been seen, and that meant that he was winning.

'It's coming!' said Pooh.

'Are you *sure* it's mine?' squeaked Piglet excitedly.

'Yes, because it's grey. A big grey one. Here it comes! A very—big—grey—Oh, no, it isn't, it's Eeyore.'

And out floated Eeyore.

'Eeyore!' cried everybody.

Looking very calm, very dignified, with his legs in the air, came Eeyore from beneath the bridge.

'It's Eeyore!' cried Roo, terribly excited.

'Is that so?' said Eeyore, getting caught up
by a little eddy, and turning slowly round three
times. 'I wondered.'

'I didn't know you were playing,' said Roo.

'I'm not,' said Eeyore.

'Eeyore, what *are* you doing there?' said
Rabbit.

'I'll give you three guesses, Rabbit. Digging holes in the ground? Wrong. Leaping from branch to branch of a young oak-tree? Wrong. Waiting for somebody to help me out of the river? Right. Give Rabbit time, and he'll always get the answer.'

'But, Eeyore,' said Pooh in distress, 'what can we—I mean, how shall we—do you think if we—'

'Yes,' said Eeyore. 'One of those would be just the thing. Thank you, Pooh.'

'He's going *round* and *round*,' said Roo, much impressed.

'And why not?' said Eeyore coldly.

'I can swim too,' said Roo proudly.

'Not round and round,' said Eeyore. 'It's much more difficult. I didn't want to come swimming at all to-day,' he went on, revolving slowly. 'But if, when in, I decide to practise a slight circular movement from right to left— or perhaps I should say,' he added, as he got into another eddy, 'from left to right, just as it happens to occur to me, it is nobody's business but my own.'

There was a moment's silence while everybody thought.

'I've got a sort of idea,' said Pooh at last, 'but I don't suppose it's a very good one.'

'I don't suppose it is either,' said Eeyore.

'Go on, Pooh,' said Rabbit. 'Let's have it.'

'Well, if we all threw stones and things into the river on *one* side of Eeyore, the stones would make waves, and the waves would wash him to the other side.'

'That's a very good idea,' said Rabbit, and Pooh looked happy again.

'Very,' said Eeyore. 'When I want to be washed, Pooh, I'll let you know.'

'Supposing we hit him by mistake?' said Piglet anxiously.

'Or supposing you missed him by mistake,' said Eeyore. 'Think of all the possibilities, Piglet, before you settle down to enjoy yourselves.'

But Pooh had got the biggest stone he could carry, and was leaning over the bridge, holding it in his paws.

'I'm not throwing it, I'm dropping it, Eeyore,'
he explained. 'And then I can't miss—I mean
I can't hit you. *Could* you stop turning round
for a moment, because it muddles me rather?'

'No,' said Eeyore. 'I *like* turning round.'

Rabbit began to feel that it was time he
took command.

'Now, Pooh,' he said, 'when I say "Now!" you can drop it. Eeyore, when I say "Now!" Pooh will drop his stone.'

'Thank you very much, Rabbit, but I expect I shall know.'

'Are you ready, Pooh? Piglet, give Pooh a little more room. Get back a bit there, Roo. Are you ready?'

'No,' said Eeyore.

'*Now!*' said Rabbit.

Pooh dropped his stone. There was a loud splash, and Eeyore disappeared . . .

It was an anxious moment for the watchers
on the bridge. They looked and looked . . . and
even the sight of Piglet's stick coming out a
little in front of Rabbit's didn't cheer them
up as much as you would have expected. And
then, just as Pooh was beginning to think that
he must have chosen the wrong stone or the
wrong river or the wrong day for his Idea,
something grey showed for a moment by the
river bank . . . and it got slowly bigger and
bigger . . . and at last it was Eeyore coming out.

With a shout they rushed off the bridge, and
pushed and pulled at him; and soon he was
standing among them again on dry land.

'Oh, Eeyore, you *are* wet!' said Piglet,
feeling him.

Eeyore shook himself, and asked somebody to
explain to Piglet what happened when you had
been inside a river for quite a long time.

'Well done, Pooh,' said Rabbit kindly. 'That
was a good idea of yours.'

'What was?' asked Eeyore.

'Hooshing you to the bank like that.'

'*Hooshing* me?' said Eeyore in surprise. 'Hooshing *me*? You didn't think I was *hooshed*, did you? I dived. Pooh dropped a large stone on me, and so as not to be struck heavily on the chest, I dived and swam to the bank.'

'You didn't really,' whispered Piglet to Pooh, so as to comfort him.

'I didn't *think* I did,' said Pooh anxiously.

'It's just Eeyore,' said Piglet. '*I* thought your Idea was a very good Idea.'

Pooh began to feel a little more comfortable, because when you are a Bear of Very Little Brain, and you Think of Things, you find sometimes that a Thing which seemed very Thingish inside you is quite different when it gets out into the open and has other people looking at it. And, anyhow, Eeyore *was* in the river, and now he *wasn't*, so he hadn't done any harm.

'How did you fall in, Eeyore?' asked Rabbit, as he dried him with Piglet's handkerchief.

'I didn't,' said Eeyore.

'I was BOUNCED,' said Eeyore.

'Oh,' said Roo excitedly, 'did somebody push you?'

'Somebody BOUNCED me. I was just thinking by the side of the river—thinking, if any of you know what that means—when I received a loud BOUNCE.'

'Oh, Eeyore!' said everybody.

'Are you sure you didn't slip?' asked Rabbit wisely.

'Of course I slipped. If you're standing on the slippery bank of a river, and somebody BOUNCES you loudly from behind, you slip. What did you think I did?'

'But who did it?' asked Roo.

Eeyore didn't answer.

'I expect it was Tigger,' said Piglet nervously.

'But, Eeyore,' said Pooh, 'was it a Joke, or an Accident? I mean—'

'I didn't stop to ask, Pooh. Even at the very bottom of the river I didn't stop to say to myself, "*Is* this a Hearty Joke, or is it the Merest Accident?" I just floated to the surface, and said to myself, "It's wet." If you know what I mean.'

'And where was Tigger?' asked Rabbit.

Before Eeyore could answer, there was a loud noise behind them, and through the hedge came Tigger himself.

'Hallo, everybody,' said Tigger cheerfully.

'Hallo, Tigger,' said Roo.

Rabbit became very important suddenly.

'Tigger,' he said solemnly, 'what happened just now?'

'Just when?' said Tigger a little uncomfortably.

'When you bounced Eeyore into the river.'

'I didn't bounce him.'

'You bounced me,' said Eeyore gruffly.

'I didn't really. I had a cough, and I happened to be behind Eeyore, and I said "*Grrrr—oppp—ptschschschz*".'

'Why?' said Rabbit, helping Piglet up, and dusting him. 'It's all right, Piglet.'

'It took me by surprise,' said Piglet nervously.

'That's what I call bouncing,' said Eeyore. 'Taking people by surprise. Very unpleasant habit. I don't mind Tigger being in the Forest,' he went on, 'because it's a large Forest, and there's plenty of room to bounce in it. But I don't see why he should come into *my* little corner of it, and bounce there. It isn't as if there was anything very wonderful about my little corner. Of course for people who like cold, wet, ugly bits it *is* something rather

special, but otherwise it's just a corner, and if anybody feels bouncy—'

'I didn't bounce, I coughed,' said Tigger crossly.

'Bouncy or coffy, it's all the same at the bottom of the river.'

'Well,' said Rabbit, 'all I can say is— well, here's Christopher Robin, so *he* can say it.'

Christopher Robin came down from the Forest to the bridge, feeling all sunny and careless, and

just as if twice nineteen didn't matter a bit,
as it didn't on such a happy afternoon, and he
thought that if he stood on the bottom rail
of the bridge, and leant over, and watched the
river slipping slowly away beneath him, then he
would suddenly know everything that there was
to be known, and he would be able to tell Pooh,
who wasn't quite sure about some of it. But
when he got to the bridge and saw all the
animals there, then he knew that it wasn't that
kind of afternoon, but the other kind, when
you wanted to *do* something.

'It's like this, Christopher Robin,' began
Rabbit. 'Tigger—'

'No, I didn't,' said Tigger.

'Well, anyhow, there I was,' said Eeyore.

'But I don't think he meant to,' said Pooh.

'He just *is* bouncy,' said Piglet, 'and he
can't help it.'

'Try bouncing *me*, Tigger,' said Roo eagerly.
'Eeyore, Tigger's going to try *me*. Piglet, do
you think—'

'Yes, yes,' said Rabbit, 'we don't all want to speak at once. The point is, what does Christopher Robin think about it?'

'All I did was I coughed,' said Tigger.

'He bounced,' said Eeyore.

'Well, I sort of boffed,' said Tigger.

'Hush!' said Rabbit, holding up his paw. 'What does Christopher Robin think about it all? That's the point.'

'Well,' said Christopher Robin, not quite sure what it was all about. '*I* think'—

'Yes?' said everybody.

'*I* think we all ought to play Poohsticks.'

So they did. And Eeyore, who had never played it before, won more times than anybody else; and Roo fell in twice, the first time by accident and the second time on purpose, because he suddenly saw Kanga coming from the Forest, and he knew he'd have to go to bed anyhow. So then Rabbit said he'd go with them; and Tigger and Eeyore went off together, because Eeyore wanted to tell Tigger How to

Win at Poohsticks, which you do by letting
your stick drop in a twitchy sort of way, if you
understand what I mean, Tigger; and
Christopher Robin and Pooh and Piglet were
left on the bridge by themselves.

For a long time they looked at the river
beneath them, saying nothing, and the river said
nothing too, for it felt very quiet and peaceful
on this summer afternoon.

'Tigger is all right, *really*,' said Piglet
lazily.

'Of course he is,' said Christopher Robin.

'Everybody is *really*,' said Pooh. 'That's
what *I* think,' said Pooh. 'But I don't suppose
I'm right,' he said.

'Of course you are,' said Christopher Robin.